My Very Very Very Very Very Very Very SILLY BOOK of GAMES

MATT LUCAS

ILLUSTRATED BY SARAH HORNE

D0319084

hello and welcome to my very very very very very very very silly book of games which i am sure you will agree is one of the best books ever written well ok maybe its not as good as harry potter and the philosophers thingy but its still pretty good and this book is full of games you can actually play whereas harry potter and the philosophers wotsit only has quidditch in it and you need a flying broomstick for that one so you cant even play it unless you are a wizard so whats the point ok maybe if you are a wasp and you have a cocktail stick that might work anyway as i say welcome to my book

Games are about HAVING FUN. The games in this book also want you to be very, very, very, very, very, very, *very* SILLY!

Even when you're being SILLY, make sure you're being SAFE. That means absolutely no knife-throwing, fire-eating or dragon-taming unless properly supervised by a qualified circus professional.

Be a good sport - win, lose or draw, be kind to your fellow players. No sulking, gloating, name-calling or tongue-sticking-out, no matter the result. And no storming out of the room and slamming the door because, remember, doors have feelings too.

Hello, These Are the Contents

GAMES TO PLAY WITH LOTS AND LOTS OF PEOPLE

if you are with a group of lots and lots of people and everyone is paying attention and people dont keep wandering off to the toilet or running around or showing someone a video on their phones and you can actually get everyone to shut up for a minute and listen then here are some games you can play

HANG ON.

LOTS and LOTS of people?

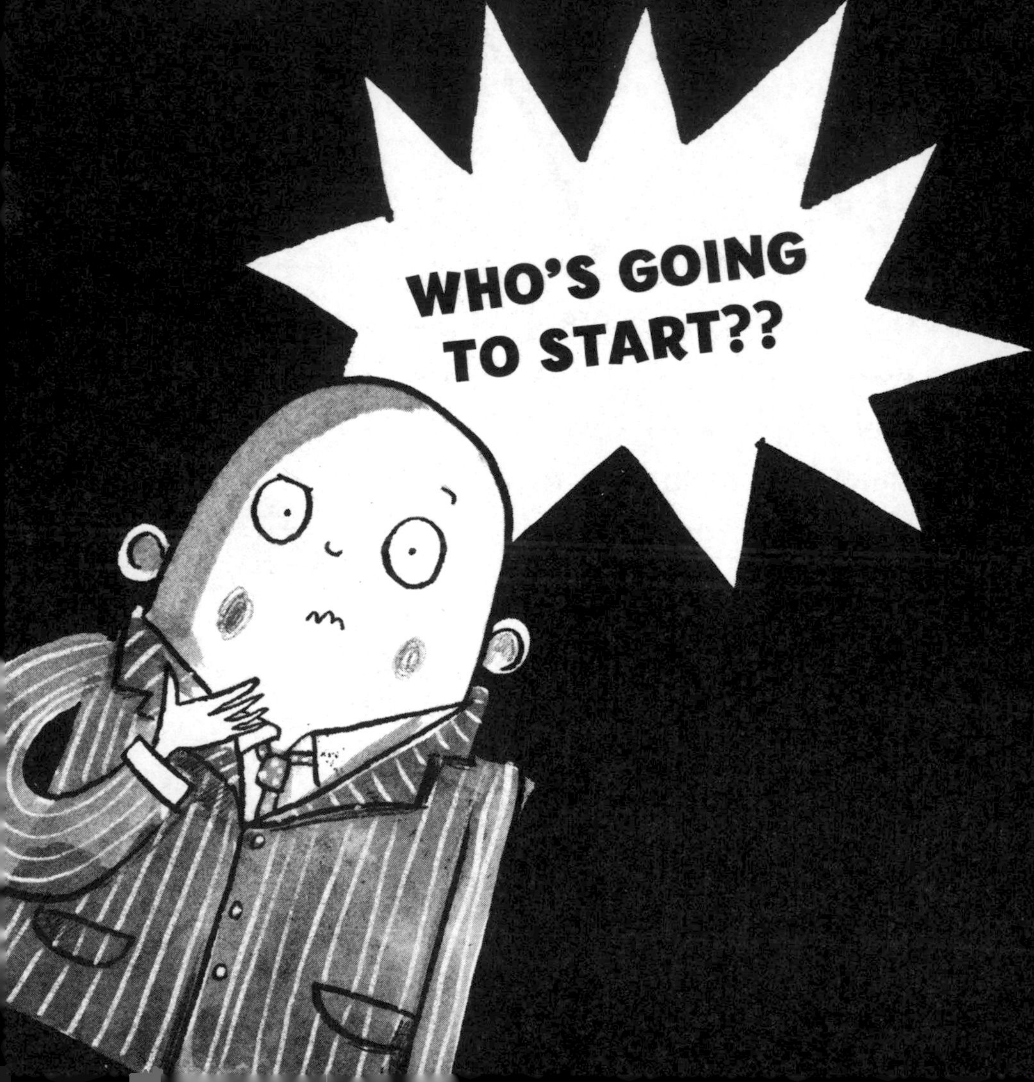

Buurrrppp

SILLY STARTERS

Lots of games start with one person being 'it'. But **WHO** is it going to be?! Here are some fun ways to decide!

★ Roll a dice, whoever gets a 6 first goes first.

★ Flip a coin – heads you get first go.

★ Play Paper, Scissors, Stone (see page 113).

★ Pick the youngest or oldest person in the group, or the person whose name begins with the earliest or latest letter of the alphabet, or who has the longest or shortest hair, or who has the most pets, or who can do the most burps in a minute . . .

What other **silly** ways can you think of?

are you ready for some games?

THE CHOCOLATE GAME

This is the **SILLIEST** game I have ever come across. You need a few things to begin:

★ A large bar of chocolate
★ A table knife and fork
★ A plate
★ A hat, gloves and scarf
★ Two dice

Are you ready? Place the chocolate, knife and fork on the plate in the centre, next to the clothes. Sit in a circle and take it in turns to roll the dice. Rolling a double (for example, two 5s) means it's your turn to play. **IMPORTANT:** everyone else keeps rolling the dice in turn.

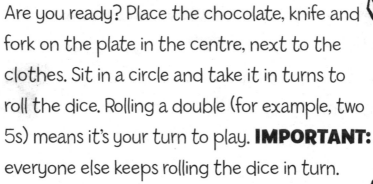

Once you've rolled a double, hurry into the middle of the circle. **Seriously! HURRY!**

12

As quick as you can, get dressed in the hat, scarf and gloves, then eat the chocolate with the knife and fork. Sounds easy? It's **NOT!** Because as soon as someone else rolls a double, it's their turn!

A very, very, very, very, very, very, *very* silly note: obviously rolling dice is, like, down to maths and stuff, but sometimes doubles come up **SURPRISINGLY LOADS**. You might want to change it so it's **ONLY** a double 6 that allows you to play. Oh, and make it fancy dress if you like. The sillier, the better!

The game ends when all the chocolate is gone. (Unless you have more chocolate!)

i love chocolate but why do they call them funsize Mars bars it would be a lot more fun if they were bigger

the way to win this game is to actually go to sleep although then you might dream that you lost the game and then you might wake up and then you would lose the game so actually ignore that

SLEEPING LIONS

All this talk of games has made me veeerrryyy sleepy . . . Luckily, here's the perfect game!

Pick two hunters. Everyone else is a sleeping lion and must lie down on the floor and NOT MOVE OR MAKE A SOUND. **Shh! I'm listening!**

The hunters start to prowl. Their aim is to wake the lions. The hunters must NOT TOUCH the lions but they can do ANYTHING ELSE to make them move or make a sound. So crack out your best jokes NOW! Any lion who moves or giggles becomes a hunter until there is only one lion left.

PIN THE TAIL ON THE DONKEY

A classic party game. But don't wait till you're having a party - play it any time!

To begin, you need a donkey. No! Kidding! You just need:

★ A picture of a donkey

★ Lots of donkey 'tails' (these could be paper or ribbon with sticky bits on the end)

★ A blindfold

One by one, players are given a donkey tail to hold, then they're blindfolded and spun around. NOW they have to try to pin the tail on the donkey. The tail that's closest to the donkey's bottom wins!

Even sillier? *Say it's Mother's Day and your mum's a gardener, change the game to 'Pin the caterpillar on the lettuce' or if it's your big brother's birthday, make it 'Pin the fart on the bum'.*

MUSICAL MAYHEM

I don't know about you, but in my opinion the best games start with music.

MUSICAL CHAIRS

Set out as many chairs as people playing. Start the music! Boogie around those chairs! When the music STOPS, everyone has to sit on a chair. Repeat, removing one chair each time until there's only one chair and one winner.

BUT WAIT, I DON'T HAVE ANY CHAIRS! No problem, you can play . . .

MUSICAL STATUES

This time when the music stops, you FREEZE. (I see you moving. Blinking counts . . . YES, REALLY!*) Anyone who moves is OUT. Repeat until only one freezer (I mean, dancer) is left.

*Not really.

before playing this game do make sure your room has a floor because if it doesnt you may fall through the centre of the earth and land in australia

BUT WAIT, FREEZING IS TOO HARD!
OK, you're being a bit difficult now.
I guess you COULD try . . .

MUSICAL BUMPS
When the music stops, you have to BUMP your BUM on the floor. Last one down is out . . . till there's only one bum on the floor.

BUT MY BUM IS SORE.
Oh . . . you can be the DJ.

WAIT, MY PARTY IS ONLINE!
No problem! Turn the page to play . . .

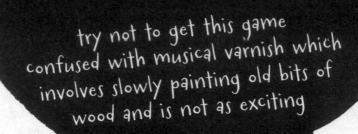

try not to get this game confused with musical varnish which involves slowly painting old bits of wood and is not as exciting

MUSICAL VANISH!

This is so much fun to play online!
When the music stops, everyone has to hide off screen. Anyone still visible is **OUT!**

And there are lots more silly games to play online:

SHOW AND SEEK

A memory game! One person begins by showing their mystery object. The next person has to remember that object and add their own. Keep going until someone forgets an object!

GO FETCH

Take it in turns to send your friends looking for things in their houses. The sillier the better! Start with something like, 'You have 30 seconds to come back wearing a hat'. Then let the searches get sillier and sillier! You could also try a rainbow hunt – come back with an object for each colour of the rainbow.

BUG UNDER THE RUG

Everyone needs:

★ A mystery object

★ A rug (or a scarf/towel/blanket)

you can play these games on your tablet but make sure you dont accidentally swallow it ha ha

Take it in turns to hide your mystery object under your rug or blanket. Your friends have to guess what's underneath!

19

DETECTIVE

Everybody in a circle? Good. Let 'The Case of the Wink Murders' begin!

Start with three people: a detective, the first victim and the murderer. Send the detective out of the room, then pick the murderer and the first victim (who lies down in the middle of the circle). The crime scene is ready!

Bring back the detective, who tries to guess the murderer while they continue to 'murder' people by **WINKING** at them. Victims must *'die'* **A DRAMATIC DEATH** in the middle of the circle. Once the detective has solved the case, the first victim becomes the next detective.

dont play this game with someone who accidentally got sunscreen in their eye because they will keep blinking and everyone in the room will be wink murdered in like five seconds even the detective themself

SpIES

Shh! Secret mission alert. You are now a covert agent tailing a suspicious spy.

OK, wait . . . first we need to pick someone to be the suspicious spy.

Done. Now, follow the spy around the room. Whenever the spy turns around, freeze as if you're part of the furniture. Like, pretend to be . . . *a bin.* The spy will interrogate you. And the questioning can be **TOUGH.** For example . . . 'You look like a spy,' the spy will say.

'Not at all,' you might reply. 'I am clearly a bin.' And you must try to look like a bin. Or a lamppost, or a bench. So how does the spy catch you out? If you unfreeze, or giggle, or if you **DON'T ACTUALLY LOOK LIKE A BIN! GAH!**

WHAT'S THE TIME, MR WOLF?

Who wants to be Mr Wolf first? You? Great!
Go and stand at the other end of the room
and turn around.

Mark a 'safe' line at the other end of the room.
Everyone else stands behind the line and shouts,
What's the time, Mr Wolf? The wolf will say
a time – like, **'3 o'clock!'** – and the rest of the
group walks three steps towards the wolf.

Repeat until the wolf says . . . **'DINNER TIME!'**
Then the wolf turns around and chases everyone
towards the 'safe' line. Whoever Wolf catches first
is the next wolf.

i wonder what would happen if you went up to a actual real genuine proper wolf and asked the time thinking about it i would imagine it would depend on whether the wolf had a watch or not

GRANDMOTHER'S FOOTSTEPS

A similar game, with Grandmother as the star!

Grandmother stands facing the wall at one end of the room, while everyone else creeps silently towards her. If you can tap Grandmother on the shoulder before she turns around, you **WIN.** The tricky thing is, Grandmother can turn around at **ANY** point, and then you have to freeze! If Grandmother spots you moving, you're out and everyone goes back to the start and tries again.

Even sillier? Lay out items of clothing on the floor. Try and get dressed while creeping. The one who puts on the most items of clothing wins!

if you dont have a grandmother maybe just ask your grandfather to wear a nightie im sure he wont mind

PARACHUTE GAMES

So, you need a parachute or large sheet for this. All the games start with the parachute spread riiiiight out on the floor and everyone sitting around it. Ready?

MUSHROOM

Everyone holds the edge of the parachute and lifts it above their heads so it makes a mushroom shape in the air. Run around under the mushroom. Or play tag, or whatever you like . . . until the mushroom falls down on you!

you have to make sure you do a really big mushroom shape or you may find there isnt mushroom for any of you ha ha do you get it

CAT AND MOUSE

The 'mouse' hides under the parachute and the 'cat' sits on top. The cat has to catch the mouse. Everyone round the edge ripples the parachute to try to help the mouse escape!

UNDER THE SEA

Hide some *treasure* under the parachute while it's still on the floor. Then send 'divers' in to get specific things while everyone else round the edges makes waves with the parachute.

NUMBERS

Number everyone 1 to 5 around the circle. Call '3' and all '3's run in while the parachute is up.

LEFT! RIGHT! LEFT!

Tell everyone to walk left, then quick turn and change direction to go right. Try not to bump into anyone!

for an extra bit of fun why not try playing this game with real ducks and geese actually no thinking about it it probably wouldnt work because they would probably just see a bit of bread somewhere and get distracted ok forget that

DUCK, DUCK, GOOSE

Another circle game – and this one's a quacker!

Everybody sits in a circle. One person starts walking round the outside, tapping people **(GENTTTLLY!)** on the head saying *'duck'* until they pick one who is the 'goose'. The goose gets up and they both race around the outside of the circle to the empty spot. Whoever is left standing starts with *'duck'* again! **QUACK!**

Even sillier? *Choose two different animals!*

PAIRS, SCISSORS, CROSSED

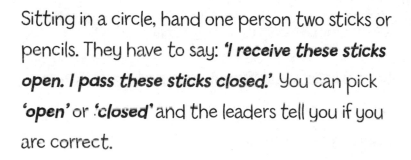

This game works best when only one or two people know how it's supposed to be played! They're the leaders. Ready?

Sitting in a circle, hand one person two sticks or pencils. They have to say: *'I receive these sticks open. I pass these sticks closed.'* You can pick *'open'* or *'closed'* and the leaders tell you if you are correct.

The secret is . . . it's nothing to do with how you pass the sticks – it's how you're sitting! If you've got your legs crossed, then **'closed'** is correct. If you're sitting with your legs out, then it's **'open'!**

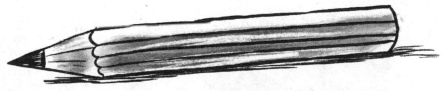

SIMON (OR) SIMONE SAYS

This one's harder than it looks . . . teehee!

Simon (or Simone) tells everyone else what do and if you don't do the thing they tell you, you're out. **BUT** Simon (or Simone) must say, *'Simon says'*.

So, if Simon says: *'Simon says put your hands on your head'*, then you have to put your hands on your head.

But if Simon just says, *'Put your hands on your head'*, then you **DON'T DO IT.** (He hasn't said *'Simon says'*.)

If you **DO** do it, then you're out.

Get it?!

simon says READ ALL OF MY BOOKS

Hi there,
I'm new.

You don't know
anyone either?

Will you be my
friend? High-five!

How do we make
friends with everyone
else?

An ICE-BREAKER GAME? Sure,
I know loads of those! How about . . .

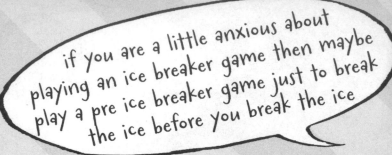

if you are a little anxious about playing an ice breaker game then maybe play a pre ice breaker game just to break the ice before you break the ice

ICE-BREAKER GAMES

ZIP, ZAP, BOING

Stand in a circle. The first player sends an invisible 'ball of energy' to someone else. A **ZIP** goes left – hold your hands out in front of you and say *'ZIP'*. A **ZAP** goes right. A **BOING** goes across the circle. Now go *FASTER! FASTER! FASTER!*

NUMBER BALL

Give everyone in the circle a number. Say the number of your friend **BEFORE** you throw the ball to them. Catch people out by looking the wrong way as you say their number. **Teehee!**

they played this game in The Sound of Music which is my favourite film apart from the bits where they keep singing and also some of the other bits

COOKIE JAR

Get a cookie jar. Everyone eats cookies. **Nom nom nom.** Best game ever. No, wait, there is an **ACTUAL** game called Cookie Jar . . .

Pass this silly rhyme around the circle.

Layla is sitting next to Leo. She says: *'Leo stole the cookie from the cookie jar.'*

Leo replies: *'Not I stole the cookie from the cookie jar.'*

Layla: *'Yes, YOU stole the cookie from the cookie jar.'*

Leo: *'Not ME!'*

Layla: *'Not YOU?'*

Leo: *'Couldn't have been!'*

Layla: *'Then WHO?'*

Leo turns to his left and begins again with: *'Lily stole the cookie from the cookie jar . . .'*

REPEAT!

TWO TRUTHS AND A LIE

Taking it in turns, each person says three things about themselves. Two must be true, and everyone has to guess which is the lie! For example:

★ I am over one metre tall.

★ I have brown eyes.

★ I have been to the Moon.

GUESS THE LIE!

WHERE DO YOU STAND?

Divide your room or play area into two. The leader calls out two options and everyone has to RUN to their choice. Like:

★ Cats left, dogs right!

★ Favourite ice-cream flavour: chocolate left, strawberry right!

★ Best sport: football left, swimming right!

32

THE SILLIEST GAMES IN THE WORLD

i dont need to tell you what is in this chapter because it does exactly what it says on the tin though i dont have the tin any more i left it on the bus along with the rest of my shopping no soup for me tonight i guess

33

Name: TOE WRESTLING

Origin: 1974, Staffordshire, England

How to play: Players take off their shoes and wrestle those big toes! Competitors give themselves SUPER SILLY names like 'The Toeminator' and 'Twinkle Toes'.

Try this at home rating: 10/10 – what are you waiting for? Get your toes out!

Name: Bog Snorkelling

Origin: 1985, Llanwyrtd Wells, Wales

How to play: You've guessed it! Snorkel through a bog . . . a peat bog to be exact! BUT you can't do usual swimming strokes, you can only use your flippers to paddle with!

Try this at home rating: 1/10 – use a bath? It won't be quite the same but . . .

Name: GIANT PUMPKIN KAYAKING

Origin: 1999, Nova Scotia, Canada

How to play: Get a giant pumpkin. No, really!
They can grow up to 500kg (yeah, that's as heavy
as an actual camel. Or a grand piano!). Hollow it
out. Get in the pumpkin and kayak it across a lake!

Even sillier? Sillier than paddling in
a giant pumpkin?! What do you take me for?
A giant tomato?

Try this at home rating: 6/10 -
see what you can do with
a NORMAL-sized
pumpkin in
the bath!

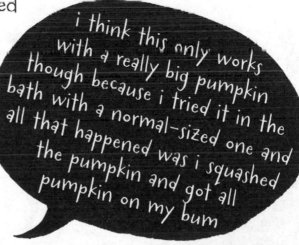

i think this only works
with a really big pumpkin
though because i tried it in the
bath with a normal-sized one and
all that happened was i squashed
the pumpkin and got all
pumpkin on my bum

cheese is my most worst food in the world ugh it tastes of yuk i would rather eat a 300 year old shoe ok thats ridiculous a 200 year old shoe then

Name: CHEESE ROLLING

Origin: 15th century Gloucestershire, England

How to play: On May bank holiday, competitors gather at Cooper's Hill in Gloucestershire. A 3-4kg Double Gloucester cheese is set off rolling down the hill and then **GO!** Everyone chases after it. Whoever reaches the finish line first wins the cheese.

Silliest fact: Cheese can reach up to 70mph racing downhill! That's as fast as a cheetah.

Try this at home rating: 7/10 - as long as you use a hard, round cheese. Cream cheese doesn't roll very well. Hmm . . .

Name: EGG THROWING

Origin: 1322, Lincolnshire, England

How to play: In teams of two, throw an egg as far as you can for someone else to catch - without breaking it.

Silliest fact: It began when an abbot encouraged his villagers to come to church by giving them each an egg. One day, the river flooded so the monks threw eggs over the water to the people. An egg-cellent sport was born!

Even sillier? According to the World Egg Throwing Federation, the world record throw is 71.2m. That's the length of a tennis court!

Try this at home rating: 0/10 - cook something delicious with your eggs instead!

Name: COMPETITIVE SLEEPING

Origin: 1998, California, USA

How to play: At events organised by the Competitive Sleep League, sleepers (or 'sleepletes') compete to see who can sleep the longest AND not get woken up by loud noises! **Yes – really!**

Try this at home rating: Sorry, I was asleep. Zzzzzzzzzz.

i once slept for nine whole months but it was inside my mums tummy ha ha so maybe i did wake up at a few points when she ate something nice so i could have a bit myself

Name: TRACTOR PULLING

Origin: 1929, Missouri and Ohio, USA

How to play: Tractors race to pull a sledge carrying heavy weights over a 100m race course.

Try this at home rating: 4/10 – just say 'Vroom' and you're a human tractor!

Name: LAWN MOWER RACING

Origin: 1963, Indiana, USA

How to play: Get on a lawn mower and RACE!

Silliest fact: Lawn mowers can reach up to 50km/h. That grass had better be scared!

Try this at home rating:
0/10 – don't!

if you dont own a lawnmower you can still cut the grass all you need is a pair of child-friendly scissors and about 40 years

Name: MUD PIT BELLY FLOPPING

Origin: 1996, Georgia, USA

How to play: Flop belly-first into a pit of mud. Loudest crowd cheer wins!

Silliest fact: Other games played at the same silly games day included toilet-seat throwing and the armpit serenade. That's when you make farty noises with your hand in your armpit. Tuneful **yuck!**

Try this at home rating: 10/10 - no, you can't do bog-snorkelling but you CAN make armpit music!

some people pay a lot of money to get covered in mud apparently it is quite good for your skin or something maybe someone should tell my mum that because whenever i come home with mud on me she starts shouting about the cost of Persil

Name: HOBBY HORSE GYMKHANA

Origin: 1990s, Finland

How to play:
Competitors jump over obstacles and perform dressage routines to music, just like at real-horse gymkhanas.

Silliest fact: The hobby horses must be given names and breeds. Giddy up, Sugarlump!

Even sillier? Oh, yes! At the *Horseless Horse Show,* the 'riders' compete on their own two feet, no horses in sight!

Try this at home rating: 10/10 - this sport was literally invented at home. Make a course out of cushions and off you go - neiiiigggh!

More super silly games from around the world:

PEA SHOOTING (England) – ready, steady, PEAAAS!

DUNNY DERBY (Australia) – aka **Toilet Racing!** Players compete in three-person teams, one sitting on a toilet, two pushing!

STAIRS-CLIMBING (global) – ow, my thighs hurt!

GURNING (England) – yeah, a world championship in pulling faces. Take that look off your face! Oh, sorry, that's just your face . . .

GAMES TO PLAY ON YOUR OWN

i done a chapter of games you can play on your own other things you can do on your own include watching telly singing lil nas x songs really loudly in the shower and picking your nose and eating it i know youre not supposed to but its quite nice if you get a crunchy one be honest

43

BALL GAMES

Ball games are all team sports, right? WRONG!
You can have all kinds of silly fun on your own.

FOOTIE FUN

If you have a football, start with keepy-uppy.
Once you get good at bouncing the ball on
your feet, move on to advanced keepy-uppy
using your knees, or behind your back, or kicking
against a wall (as long as the wall does not include
a breakable window or an angry grown-up).

Did you know, in America they call keepy-uppy
'hacky sack' and they use a little bean bag instead
of a ball!

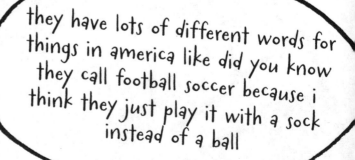

they have lots of different words for things in america like did you know they call football soccer because i think they just play it with a sock instead of a ball

TREMENDOUS TENNIS

If tennis is more your thing, get super silly with your racket tricks. Yes, you can bounce the ball against a wall (see note on non-grumpy walls) – that's easy, but can you:

1. bounce it ON your racket
2. bounce and spin yourself around before the ball comes down
3. bounce and spin your racket around before the ball comes down
4. use TWO rackets and bounce the ball through your legs like a basketball . . .?

Hmm.

1.

2.

3.

4.

HULA HOOP

Already an expert at ball tricks? How's your hula game? The world record holder, Marawa Ibrahim from Australia, can get up to 200 hoops spinning on herself at once!

thats nothing i once ate four bags of Hula Hoops in one sitting

SKATING, ROLLING, BLADING HULA HOOP

If you've got a skateboard, rollerskates, rollerblades or even a scooter, you can practise some sweet silly tricks. And get to the shops faster to get some sweets. Win win!

JUGGLING

The silliest skill of all! You'll need three small, soft balls. Start by throwing and catching just one. Then try two at once: holding one ball in each hand, throw Ball One up, and as it's coming down, throw Ball Two up.

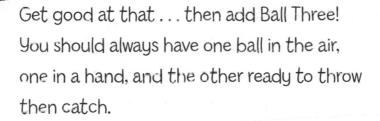

Get good at that . . . then add Ball Three! You should always have one ball in the air, one in a hand, and the other ready to throw then catch.

NOW COMES THE SILLY PART. Juggle with anything you like. (As long as you're in a safe place and nothing is breakable – you don't want to bonk yourself or anyone else on the head!)

i really want to get better at juggling but its hard juggling that with all the other circus skills i am trying to learn

AIM GAMES

There are lots of throwing or rolling game kits you can easily play solo, like boules, quoits, skittles or bowling. If you don't have a set, you can easily make one. And why not make it SILLY!

SILLY SKITTLES

Collect six empty loo rolls, ball up some scrap paper and you've got a skittle set! **OR** you could use empty plastic bottles. You could decorate the bottles as something you'd want to knock down. No, **NOT** your brother! Like, one could be **'homework'** and another could be **'broccoli'.** The sillier the better!

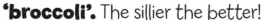

if you dont have six empty loo rolls just eat lots and lots and lots of spaghetti and then do a really big poo and that should speed things up

MARBLES

You can play this classic game with other people, but if you play for 'keeps' (you win any marbles you knock out of the circle), you'd better practise on your own first!

★ Pick a 'shooter' marble (a big one is best).
★ Draw a circle on the ground.
★ Put 10-15 marbles in the middle of the circle.
★ Stand a few feet away.
★ Flick your shooter marble into the circle.
Any marbles that go outside the line, you win!
(Always take care not to let little siblings near your marbles.)

MORE MARBLE FUN: make marble mini golf or a marble pinball using an old shoebox.

But remember - DON'T LOSE YOUR MARBLES!

PAPER AEROPLANES

How far can you throw a paper aeroplane? More importantly, how AWESOME an aeroplane can you make?

1. Start with an A4 sheet of paper. Fold it in half lengthways.
2. Open out the paper and fold the bottom two corners into the centre line.
3. Fold the 'new' corners into the centre line.
4. Fold the plane in half lengthways again.
5. Fold each wing in half.
6. Ta-da! Now give your plane an awesome name!

Tip: planes fly faster with a slim nose and bigger wings.

please make sure you read this properly and dont make a pooper aeroplane ha ha ha ew

1.
2.
3.
4.
5.
6.

im not very good at this i might skip this one

SKIPPING SKILLS

Got a skipping rope? Got an outdoor space where you're not going to lasso anyone? Great! And once you've had some practice, grab a friend or two and skip together.

Here are some super **silly** skipping challenges:

★ Count how many skips you can do in a minute.

★ Skip on one foot then the other.

★ Flip the rope from side to side between skips.

★ Cross your arms in and out.

★ Cross your legs in and out.

★ Turn a full circle while skipping.

★ Do a handstand then get back to skipping.

★ **JUGGLE WHILE SKIPPING.**

Kidding. But did you know **BOXERS** love to skip as part of their workouts?

★ Skip on your bum. **Yes really!** There's a world record for this: 115 bum skips in a minute – beats the bumps!

Oh, sorry,
we skipped
a page.

HAHAHAHA!

A TOUCH OF MAGIC!

Do you have a pack of cards? You can
have HOURS of fun polishing your
magic tricks ready to wow a crowd.
Why not start with . . .

SILLY SHUFFLES

Every magician needs to know how to **shuffle**.
Start by taking a wedge of cards from the
back of the pack and popping it in the front.
Keep going till the pack is nicely mixed. Then
split the deck in two. Holding one half in each
hand, thumbs close together on the corners,
ripple the cards into each other. Impressive!

You can get **super silly** with this, arching
the cards so they flutter down, and even
making it look like the cards are raining!

57

PICK A CARD, ANY CARD

You've seen this, right? The magician asks you to pick a card, show it to your friends, then put it back anywhere in the pack. **SOMEHOW** the magician then guesses exactly which one your card is. **BUT HOW???**

The **silly** secret: sort the pack into one red half and one black half. Practise fanning out the cards face down, then pay careful attention to which half your friend picks their card from. Then you close up the pack and make sure they return it to the opposite half. **Be sneaky with the way you hold out the deck so they pick the half you want!**

Then when you pick up the cards, you'll see a red or black card standing out in the 'wrong' section!

You can also spend time learning some cool close-hand magic tricks like . . .

DISAPPEARING COIN

You need a coin and a top with long sleeves that come down riiiight over your wrists. Hold out both hands, palms up. Put the coin on the palm of one hand. Snap the fingers of your other hand over the coin a few times. Then, snap again, and flick the coin up your sleeve with your snapping finger. **THIS NEEDS A LOT OF PRACTICE TO MAKE IT LOOK MAGICAL AND COOL!**

if you dont have a pack of cards why not be practical and make one of your own from things you find around the house like some slices of ham, a ping pong ball and an After Eight

THE BANISH BOREDOM BOARD GAME

That's it, you've tried everything. You can pull 17 coins from behind your cat's ear. You can hula hoop for two hours with 90 hoops at once. Your skittles have run away because you've knocked them down so many times, and now you've played every card game that exists. What next?

MAKE YOUR OWN BOARD GAME!

Copy the template on pages 62 and 63 **OR** just get started with your own squares and challenges on a piece of paper.

Some things to think about . . .

What's the BIG IDEA? Is it a journey? Are players trying to find something? Is it a race?

What will your pieces be? Different coloured unicorns? All your favourite sea creatures? Vegetables with silly names?

How will your pieces move? Using rolls of the dice? A spinner? The number of star jumps each person can do in a minute?

Are there any cards for extra points or extra challenges?

And most importantly – give your game a super **silly** name!

SPOT THE ODD MATT OUT

1.

2.

3.

4.

Answer on page 80.

THE OLDEST GAMES IN HISTORY

i know you probably think Sonic the Hedgehog is the oldest game in history but actually there are games that are even older than that im not even lying and you can read about some of them in this chapter if you like

BOARD GAMES

Because there was no telly, ancient people got bored so they invented board games.

One of the oldest board games in the world is called **SENET** and it's over 5,000 years old! Boards were found depicted on ancient Egyptian wall paintings and buried in tombs – including the tomb of King Tutankhamun!

No one really knows how it was played, but a board had 30 squares and player got five or more pawns (small pieces) that probably moved from square to square. The rules and pieces changed over thousands of years of play!

i thought this said five prawns and i was like oh this game is gonna make your fingers all sticky

DRAUGHTS

The earliest board was found in Ur, in what's now Iraq, in around 3000BCE. Players take each other's pieces by moving across the board. Gotcha!

MANCALA

An ancient African game, where the marbles or stones are moved across little holes in a board.

NINE MEN'S MORRIS

This one's a bit like NOUGHTS AND CROSSES. In medieval England, some villages made giant boards, using people as moving pieces!

BACKGAMMON

Super old and super complicated.

apparently this game got its name because the man who invented it carried some gammon around on his back in case he got hungry ha ha not really

GREEKS AND ROMANS

Kids in ancient times had **LOTS** of fun. Ancient Greek children played **MARBLES, HOPSCOTCH** and **LEAPFROG**, as well as **KNUCKLEBONES.** (They used real bones, not plastic tacks like we have today - ugh!) Another cool game was **EPHEDRISMOS**, a kind of a team piggyback race. Why not give it a go - make up your own rules!

They also played **YO-YO, SKIPPING** and pretend **CHARIOT RACING** with goats or dogs instead of horses. Probably don't try this at home!

VIKING FUN

You know the Vikings? Well, they liked board games. They had an early version of **CHESS**

and there is evidence of a children's game called **HNEFATAFL. (Bless you!)** Another Viking favourite was **TOGA-HONK** or **TUG-OF-WAR!** Grab your rope and **puuuuuuulll!**

INUIT GAMES

Traditionally, Inuit games taught kids useful hunting skills. Some are still played in the World Eskimo-Indian Olympics! There's **HIGH-KICK** - competing to kick very high targets - and **KNUCKLE HOP** - like long jump except you start balanced on your fists. **BLANKET TOSS** began as a way for hunters to see way into the distance: a 'rider' sitting on top of a large blanket gets 'flipped' as high as possible into the air!

i have never been to the arctic but I have reached into the back of the freezer to pull out the last Calippo and if its anything like as cold as that count me out

VICTORIAN GAMES

Good day, young urchin! In Victorian times, there were many excellent games to keep kids amused. For example, this STICK AND HOOP . . .

No, really – Victorian children **LOVED** sticks and hoops! Stick-hoop challenges included: **How Long Can You Keep It Rolling** and **How Far Can You Roll It! EPIIIIIC!** They also enjoyed **DIABOLO** – a spool with a string tied between two ropes. You can do all kinds of tricks with them!

they had to play games in victorian times because there was no TikTok but if there was it probably would have been people lipsyncing to nursery rhymes while up a chimney

In the market for a smaller Victorian toy? How about a **SPINNING TOP** or a **YO-YO?** Yes, yo-yos have existed for centuries!

If you were a wealthy Victorian child, you might even have enjoyed a fancy new invention – the **LEATHER FOOTBALL**. Before this, people used a ball of rags or an inflated pig's bladder as a ball. **EW! DISGUSTING!**

Even fancier? How about a home-made doll, some toy soldiers or toy tea set? Really, really, really well-off Victorian kids might even have had an **AUTOMATON** - that's like a really, really early robot toy. **Bleep! Bloop!**

FOOTBALL FUN

FOOTBALL, the beautiful game? The SILLIEST game, more like . . .

Ever since humans first walked, they have kicked . . . and played football. Well, they had to invent the ball first. And the goal. The first footie in history is the Chinese game **CUJU** from about 200BCE.

Since then, football has kept on getting sillier. Did you know . . .

In 1945, Arsenal played a game in thick fog. No one could see anything! Players who'd been sent off snuck back on. The goalkeeper ran into the post and knocked himself out. A spectator even came down from the stands to join in.

The Isles of Scilly have the silliest league – there are only two teams! They play 17 times per season to determine the winner. Then the teams play each other again in the Cup Final!

Romanian club Steaua tried to get permission to dig a **crocodile-infested moat** around their pitch to stop their fans running onto the pitch!

The fastest red card in history was **TWO SECONDS** after the starting whistle in an English Sunday League match.

And more than one in twenty injuries on the pitch are caused by celebrating goals. Hurr-ARGH!

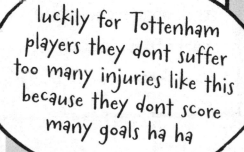

luckily for Tottenham players they dont suffer too many injuries like this because they dont score many goals ha ha

MORE SPORTS SILLINESS

Over the years, people have come up with LOTS of silly ways to make sport more fun.

Did you know that **RUGBY** is a silly version of football? At Rugby School in the 1820s, boys began to run with the ball. It wasn't allowed at first – but it caught on ... and rugby was born!

That's not the only ball sport revamp in history. **NETBALL** was invented in 1897 so that women could play **BASKETBALL** in their long skirts.

And **LACROSSE** was invented as a form of battle by native American tribes. Games could go on for days!

CRICKET still goes on for days, sometimes. The longest match ever took 12 days!

75

CHESS

**Are you a super brainy person? Yes!
Then maybe you play CHESS?**

Chess is one of the oldest board games in the world. The first recorded game was in the 10th century in Baghdad, Iraq.

In the 12th century, chess was banned by the church in France. But in 1125, one super sneaky priest who loved playing chess invented the folding board – it looked like two books lying on top of each other! Mwahah! Cool trick!

Did you know . . .

if you played human chess then you could have john bishop as one of the bishops ha ha

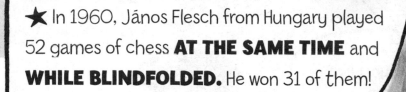

★ In 1960, János Flesch from Hungary played 52 games of chess **AT THE SAME TIME** and **WHILE BLINDFOLDED.** He won 31 of them!

★ The longest game technically possible is a yawn-inducing 5,949 moves.

★ The shortest possible win is in two moves. It's called **'Fool's Mate Run'.** Super silly!

★ Human chess - with people as the pieces - features in *Alice Through the Looking-Glass* and *Harry Potter and the Philosopher's Stone.*

★ Chess Boxing (combining chess and boxing) is another super silly way to play chess. Also - ouch.

★ The phrase **'checkmate'** comes from the Persian **'shāh māt'**, meaning 'the king is dead'.

WHICH BOARD GAME?

Do you like spelling?

NO

Indubitably!

Are you a bit of an artist?

NO

YES

How's your general knowledge?

Scrabble
You have to make words out of random letter tiles, using all kinds of double and triple letter score squares on the board. Spelling-tastic!

Pictionary
Like Charades but drawing not acting

Sign me up to *University Challenge* right now

Trivial Pursuit
Awesome general knowledge board game where you also win pieces of PIE!

Do you love Monopoly? How about the Game of Life? Or Pictionary? If it's a rainy day outside and you've got a cupboard full of games, here's a quiz to help you pick which game to play!

Good with money?

That's a bit personal

Kerching!

What about solving mysteries?

Err . . . no . . .

Monopoly
Race around town buying and selling property and trying to send your fellow players to jail. HA HA HA!

I'm a super sleuth

Cluedo
Whodunnit? You'll find out soon!

Why not read a book instead? I've got a great joke book, for example . . .

GAMES TO PLAY AT HOME

if you are at home and you
want to play some games
then why not pick up my very
very very very very very
silly book of games because
theres a whole chapter in it
on games to play at home
oh hang on youre reading it
right now sorry ignore
me i am a idiot

THE HAT GAME

Everyone writes three (or more) famous people's names on small pieces of paper and puts them in a hat. Pick teams then one person pulls a name out of the hat and describes the famous person to their team. You can't say the name or use rhyming words. How many names can your team guess correctly in two minutes?!

For **EVEN MORE FUN**, keep playing until the names run out. Then put the names back in the hat for another round. This time, you can only say **ONE WORD** to describe each person. So hopefully you have got your teammates to guess that the 'famous tennis player' is 'Serena Williams' in round one. In round two, you could just say 'tennis' and hope they remember - or guess - correctly!

82

AND THAT'S NOT ALL . . .

For round **THREE**, you're not allowed to say
ANYTHING - you can only act out the people.

This gets **super, super silly.** I challenge you
not to giggle while playing!

if you don't like this game
you can play a different
game where you just wear
a hat instead and thats all
but it does get a bit boring
after about an hour

KIM'S GAME

You'll need:

★ A tray

★ Some objects that will fit on the tray (little things like a toy car, a fork, a raisin ...)

★ A tea towel to cover the objects

★ A timer

Set up the tray of objects beforehand, then **COVER THE TRAY** so no one can see the objects. Set your timer for one minute, whip the tea towel off the tray and tell everyone to **CONCENTRATE VERY HARD** and try to remember what's on the tray. **Ding ding ding!** Time's up! Cover the tray again then ...

... take it in turns to remember what was on the tray. The person who remembers the most objects is the winner!

TREASURE HUNT

This game is almost as much fun to plan as it is to play!

The basics: hide your treasure, then leave a trail of clues to lead your friends and family to the prize! You could even make the clues rhyme. It takes time, but you'll find people, err . . .
I ran out of rhymes, sorry.

Treasure hunts are even sillier if you add a theme, like dinosaurs, monsters or unicorns.

Turn the page for a pirate-themed treasure hunt to get you st-AAARRR-ted . . .

Avast ye me hearties! This here be
a treasure hunt. Copy out the clues
and hide them for yer shipmates to find.
Don't forget to hide the treasure under
a great big X. Arrrr!

1. The trail starts here, easier than you think.
   The first clue is hidden . . . in the kitchen sink!

2. Next, I'll test your clever mind.
   Seek what gets wet . . . as it dries.

3. You found the towel! Well done, kid.
   You'll see right through where the next
   clue's hid.

4. The windowsill! Congrats, yippee.
The next clue's hiding under a tree.

5. Well done, great seeking! One more
to be got.
You will find the treasure where X
marks the spot . . .

What was your buried treasure?
Pieces of eight? A cake? (Yum, cake.)

Even sillier? Over to you! Invent your
own treasure hunt! You could use
picture clues or a map instead of words
and rhymes.

SCAVENGER HUNT

Do you like making lists? Me too!

Make a list of items for your family or friends to collect around the house. The **sillier** the better, for example:

★ Hat

★ Mat

★ Cat (it doesn't have to be a REAL cat!)

You could play outdoors and look for things like leaves and pine cones and **squirrels** (maybe just take a photo of the squirrel!).

You could also try a RAINBOW HUNT, where you have to find seven different-coloured things: red, orange, yellow, green, blue, indigo and violet.

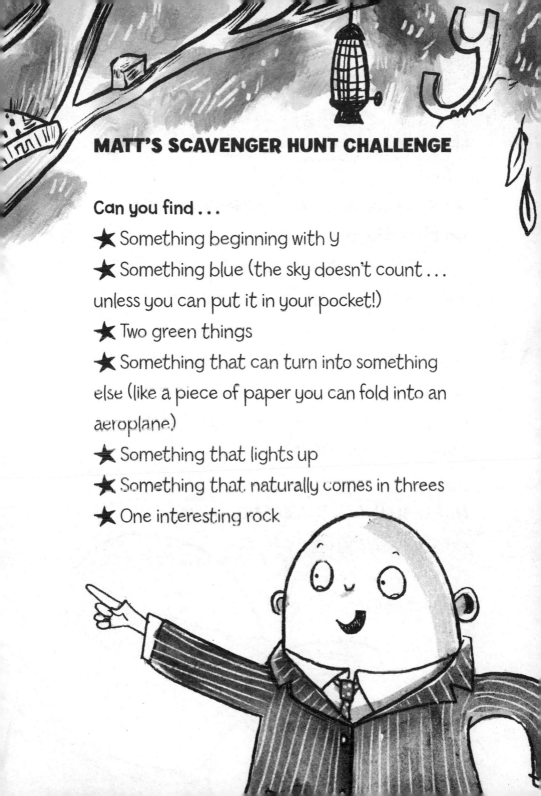

MATT'S SCAVENGER HUNT CHALLENGE

Can you find . . .

★ Something beginning with y

★ Something blue (the sky doesn't count . . .
unless you can put it in your pocket!)

★ Two green things

★ Something that can turn into something
else (like a piece of paper you can fold into an
aeroplane)

★ Something that lights up

★ Something that naturally comes in threes

★ One interesting rock

HIDE AND SEEK

I know you know this one . . .

Someone counts to ten **(cover your eyes – no cheating)** while everyone else hides. They call, *'Ready or not, here I come!'* and they go and look for you all! Last one hiding wins.

Silly it up by counting in strange leaps *(7 . . . 14 . . . 21 . . . banana)*, or dressing up as a ghost when you're hiding, then jumping out at the seeker shouting, **'BOO!'**

NOT REALLY, THAT'S CHEATING. Unless everyone playing agrees to do some silly rule-bending in the first place . . .

SARDINES

Hide and seek with a fun, fishy (I mean . . . squishy) twist!

This time, one person goes to hide, everyone else counts then you call, **'Ready or not, here we come!'** and you ALL go in different directions to look for the person hiding. If you find the hider, you hide with them. Everyone else continues to search until EVERYONE has found the secret hiding place!

Top game tips: Try to hide somewhere with plenty of space. Only so many people will fit inside a shoebox, after all.

i had a tin of sardines once it was quite nice but i did find the tin a bit chewy

POST-IT PEOPLE

Everyone writes down the name of a famous person or character on a Post-it note, then puts it on someone else's forehead without them reading it. Now you **BECOME** the person on your Post-it! Taking it in turns, ask questions about who you are. First one to guess wins!

make sure you remember to take the Post-it off your head at some point in your life obviously or people will think you are a bit odd

TWENTY QUESTIONS

This time, one player thinks of a famous person or character and everyone else has 20 questions to guess who it is. **BUT** they only get **YES OR NO ANSWERS.** It's actually trickier than it sounds!

WOULD YOU RATHER?

Take it in turns to give options – **would you rather be a dog or a cat?** Would you rather have flying or invisibility as your superpower? Would you rather never watch telly again or never eat chocolate again? You know, completely normal questions. This one is **EXCELLENT** for getting to know new friends!

TONGUE TWISTERS

You'll need a friend or sibling for these tongue-twisting challenges. Both of you hold the book and start reading the tongue twisters below **OUT LOUD** (with no mistakes!). The first one to finish slams the book shut and is the **WINNER!**

1. A wicked cricket critic.

2. Peter Piper picked a peck of pickled peppers. A peck of pickled peppers Peter Piper picked. If Peter Piper picked a peck of pickled peppers, Where's the peck of pickled peppers Peter Piper picked?

you had better get this right or you will have to eat an ice lorry ha ha

3. How much wood would a woodchuck chuck if a woodchuck could chuck wood? He would chuck, he would, as much as he could, and chuck as much wood as a woodchuck would, if a woodchuck could chuck wood

4. She sells seashells by the seashore. The shells she sells are seashells, I'm sure.

5. Red lorry, yellow lorry, red lolly, yellow lolly. Red lorry, yellow lorry, red lolly, yellow lolly.

MOUSETRAP

This is a board game, yes, BUT why not make your own version? (That's always more fun!)

Raid the recycling bin for (clean) boxes, tubes, plastic bottles or cartons you can cut holes in, and create an obstacle run for a marble. Go big!

Make it go all the way around your bedroom. Have a seesaw and a swinging post. Make it suitable for your hamster to go round . . .

Actually, please get the hamster's permission before you attempt this.

OK, I need a break after all that silliness!

Not a problem.

Let's play . . .

THE QUIET GAME

See who can stay the quietest for the longest. Sounds boring? Er . . . no! It is **AMAZING** if you have annoying younger siblings. Or **hamsters.** Hamsters always lose. It's their **squeaky** wheels.

i once had a pet hamster and he was huuuuuge but he was so clever he would come when you called him and could sit and lay down and give you his paw he must have been the cleverest hamster that ever lived honestly he was more like a dog he was amazing actually come to think of it he might have been a dog sorry ignore this

CRAZY 4 CARDS!

Got a deck of cards? You're ready to get silly! Here are a few of my favourite games . . .

SNAP

Aim: Two or more players compete to win the whole deck.

How: Split the deck equally among the players. With your piles of cards face down, take turns to turn over one card and place it quickly in the middle. When you get a matching number, the first person to slam their hand down on the pile and say, **'SNAP!'** wins all the cards. First one to snaffle the whole deck wins!

SLAM

Aim: Two players battle to lose all their cards.

How: Get down on the floor. No, really, this one gets messy! Split the deck into two. Each of you lays out four cards face up, and places the rest of your deck face down. When you're both ready, say, **'SLAM!'** and each of you puts one card from your face-down pile into the middle (lay them next to each other). Now, taking cards from your face-up row of four, start placing them on two new centre piles in number order, getting higher. You can use both piles - and keep replacing your face-up cards from your face-down pile. Keep going until you both can't go any more. Then both players say, **'Ready? SLAM!'** and turn over another card into the centre. First one to get rid of their cards wins!

GO FISH!

Aim: Two or more players aim to get rid of all their cards.

How: Deal five cards to each player and place rest of the deck face down in the middle. Starting with the player next to you, ask them for a number. Your aim is to build a set (e.g. four 9s), so only ask for a 9 if you already have one. If they have a 9, they must hand it over. Now ask the next person till no one else has a 9.

Now the fun starts! Instead of saying 'No', they say, **'GO FISH!'** Turn over the top card on the deck. If it's a 9, keep it and start asking for a new number. If it's NOT a 9, place it face up on the table and then it's the next person's go. When you have a set of four, place them face up in front of you. Keep going till one player is out of cards - the winner!

PIG!

Aim: Two or more players aim to get four of a kind.

How: Sort the deck into piles of four of a kind (e.g. four aces, four kings). Pick up as many piles as there are players, then discard the rest. SHUFFLE WELL! Now deal four cards to each player. You'll each need a piece of paper too.

First person: hand one card to your neighbour.
Next person: do the same.
Keep doing this. When you have four of a kind, put your finger on your nose. If you notice someone else with a finger on their nose, put YOUR finger on YOUR nose. The last person to put a finger on their nose loses! The loser gets a 'P' – write this down on a piece of paper. Play another round. If you got a 'P' and you lose again, you get an 'I'. Keep playing, and the first person to get P-I-G loses. **OINK!**

MEMORY GAME

Do you remember this game? Just kidding. I haven't explained it yet!

Start by saying, *'I'm going to the shops to buy . . . '* and mention one item. The next person lists your item and adds their own. Keep going and see how long a list you can remember! Make it super silly for the next person by making your item really long and complicated **(snigger!)**.

A very, very, very, very, very, very, very silly version: You don't always have go to the shops. You could go to the Moon, or on a pirate adventure. I don't know about you, but if I were going on a pirate ship, I'd probably need my parrot, cutlass, eye patch, skull and crossbones flag . . .

DOMINOES

You could play the traditional domino matching game or . . . you could create an epic domino downfall obstacle course, lining up dominos all over your room – no, all over your house – no, out of the front door . . .

Line them up, give the first one a flick and watch as they topple into an amazing domino trail!

CHALK CHALLENGES

Top tip: wait till it isn't raining to play these!

It's not only **HOPSCOTCH*** you can play on the pavement outside your house. If you have big chalk you can have big sillies outside . . .

You could draw a zigzag obstacle route, **SNAKES AND LADDERS** or even a Twister board. You could do a maze or pawprint trail. Or do sums or set people challenges like 'Gather four sticks here', or 'Sing a sunshine song'.

*But you could also play hopscotch!

Here's a super silly version . . .

MATT'S SILLY SPORTS DAY

Welcome to the silliest sports day around!
Challenge your friends and family to these
weird and wonderful events - then make up
more of your own!

JUMP FOR IT!

High? Long? Star? Who can do the most
spectacular jump without moving from the spot?

EGG AND SPOON RACE

Place one hard-boiled egg and one spoon on
the starting line. Shout **'go'** and see which
one reaches the finish line first. Ha ha!

if you want to brighten the
game up why not draw a picture
of an egg on your egg

SACK RACE

Sack race - race sacks. I mean, get in sacks and race by jumping in them!

THREE-LEGGED RACE

Tie your leg to your friend's leg - and race to the finish!

LONGEST STATUE

See who can hold still for the longest.

PET RACING

Bring your pets and race them. I'm guessing a dog would beat a hamster but there's still everything to play for. Better yet, owners race and see whose pet cheers the loudest!

MEDALS

ALL must win prizes! As well as medals for coming first, second or twenty-ninth place, give awards for best dressed, best supporter, best victory dance. **(I like the Macarena.)**

Why not perform a closing ceremony to mark the end of the day?

if someone gives you a prize for something just let them get on with it and dont meddle with the medal ha ha

GAMES TO PLAY IN THE CAR OR BUS OR TRAIN

here are some games to play
in the car or bus or train and
also now that i think about
it you could probably play
them on a plane but its too
late to change the title of
the chapter now because they
already printed it sorry

109

I SPY

Or is it Eye Spy? Hmmmmm. However it's spelled, it's the ULTIMATE car game. Enjoy!

Start by saying *'I spy with my little eye, something beginning with . . . '* and then say the first letter of the word of whatever you've spotted.

Obviously if you're on a car long journey, you'll spot cows, sheep, road signs, that kind of thing, but why not silly it up? Like *'S'* for *'sheep . . . which I can see in the clouds'*, or *'E'* for *'emerald green grass'* . . . No one will ever guess!

OK, maybe that's **CHEATING**. But **DO** look for really tricky things to find!

RACING RAINDROPS

Each pick a raindrop and race to see whose gets to the bottom of the window first. They genuinely go faster if you cheer. And give them names like **Choo Choo T-RAIN. Ha ha!**

> if it is not raining you can play with imaginary raindrops and then no one can prove you didnt win

SPOTTER'S GAME

Make your own rules for this one! Like, you could give out 5s and 10s for certain landmarks along the way. Maybe you give 5 points for a pylon or a green road sign, but 10 for a windmill or one million for an upside-down cow.

ALPHABET GAME

Honestly, you can play this one for HOURS!

Go through the alphabet and, with a different category each time, take it in turns to name something for each letter, The person who can't think of anything for their letter is out.

Vegetables: avocado, beetroot, cauliflower . . .
Fruit: apple, banana, clementine . . .
Sports: air hockey, badminton, chess . . .
Animals: antelope, baboon, **CHEESE** . . .

Wait, that's wrong. Sorry, I'm just hungry!

Animals: antelope, baboon, **CHOCOLATE** . . .

Still hungry!

PAPER, SCISSORS, STONE

Count to three, then pick your 'weapon'!

Paper covers stone - paper wins!
Stone blunts scissors - stone wins!
Scissors cut paper - scissors win!

I always play it to settle an argument.

Or to win the last slice of cake.

I always win.

ALWAYS . . .

...OH NO, I LOST!

It's OK! Just keep playing. Start with 'best of three' rounds. Then you have to win TWICE to win.

...I'M STILL LOSING!

Why not introduce your own rounds? Like, dragon breathes fire and scorches everything to win **OR** black hole sucks everything into its orbit to win. Whoosh!

...PLEASE HELP ME WIN!

Go global! This game is called Rock, Paper, Scissors in America and Schnick Schnack Schnuck in Germany! Since your opponent probably won't know those rules (hint: they're the SAME rules, just with different words), you can fool them into losing each time!

on jupiter they call it flurbidoo wipney popatop

PEN AND PAPER GAMES

WARNING! DON'T DO THESE IN THE CAR IF THEY MAKE YOU CAR SICK!

(I can play them on a plane, train or boat, but not in the car. Bleeeeeergh. What's that all about?)

NOUGHTS AND CROSSES

First one to get a row of three wins.

this is believed to be one of the first games ever invented alongside tic tac toe and Hungry Hungry Hippos which in prehistoric times was played with real hippos

BOX GAME

Play in pairs. Fill a page with evenly spaced dots in a grid – or use grid paper! Then, using different coloured pens, take it in turns to draw a single line between two dots. When you draw the fourth line to make a square, put your initial in it. The person with the most boxes at the end wins!

WORDS WITHIN WORDS

Compete to find as many different small words from a long word as possible, with a time limit. Like, from 'BUMPINESS', you can make 'bus', 'buses' and 'bum'.

SNOWMAN

Try to guess the word before the snowman is complete!

Someone thinks of a word and writes enough spaces for the letters. Everyone else guesses letters in turn. If a letter is in the word, write it on the correct space. If it's not, draw one element of the snowman.

_ N _ _ W _ A _

Even sillier? *My snowmen like to wear hats, gloves, elaborate twig moustaches and carry packed lunch boxes. It's a lot to draw. But it also gives everyone a lot more guesses . . .*

117

WORD LADDER

Changing ONLY ONE LETTER AT A TIME,
use a word to create another word of the
same length. Like . . .

RACE
RATE
MATE
MARE

CARE
CARS
CART
FART
FARM
FORM

CONSEQUENCES

Start with one piece of paper and fold it several
times, like a concertina. Open out the folds.
The first person draws the head or hat on the first
section then folds down their bit and passes it on.
The next person draws the neck or shoulders . . .
you get the idea.

At the end, unfold your bonkers mash-up picture!

**Guess what? This
game works with
WORDS too . . .**

Instead of drawing pictures, tell a silly story with everyone taking a turn. Fold the paper so that the next person can see only the END of what you've written.

Try to leave your sentence 'hanging' or unfinished. So, instead of writing *And the penguins all went home to bed*, you could write '*And the penguins all went . . .*' and see what the next person writes! Here's an example:

Once upon a time, an evil wizard . . .

. . . turned my best friend Sami into a . . .

. . . very big and slimy frog and he . . .

. . . lived on a spaceship where he was in charge of . . .

. . . counting stars because he was very very . . .

... hungry so he asked the Chief Spider to ...

... sing a lovely song and she said ...

... Oops, I just farted and then ...

... everyone cheered and then they ...

... went to bed because it was the morning ...

... the end ...

... or is it?

GET-TO-KNOW-YOU-BINGO

Give everyone a piece of paper with nine or more boxes on, each with a fact in it. Now start talking to people to tick them off the bingo card. First person with names in each box wins! Here's an example:

WE HAVE A CAT AT HOME.	I WEAR GLASSES.	I LIKE PICKLES.
I AM GOOD AT MATHS.	I HAVE BROWN HAIR.	I AM WEARING SOCKS.
MY FAVOURITE TEA IS CHIPS AND KETCHUP.	I EAT SLUGS.	MY FAVOURITE ANIMAL IS AN ELEPHANT.

GAMES TO WEAR YOU OUT

parents love their kids playing these sorts
of games because after you play them you
are really really tired and although your
parents love you lots and lots they love
you even more when you have an early
night because it means they get to watch
all those television shows with rude words
in them

RUN AROUND

Are you feeling energetic? Good. Here's the BEST AND MOST ACTIVE QUIZ EVER!

Name four corners or spots on a field as A, B, C and D. You'll need to choose a quizmaster who asks questions with four different answers. If you think the answer is *'B'*, you **LEG IT** to corner B. Whoever gets it wrong is out. Or you just run back to the middle and keep playing. **FOR EVER.**

A colourful version: instead of numbers, give each corner the name of a colour. Then ask questions where the answer is one of those colours. So . . . *'What colour is a fire engine?'* and you all **RUN** to the **RED** corner.

RED LIGHT, GREEN LIGHT

One person becomes the traffic light. Everyone else runs around. The traffic light yells, *'RED LIGHT!'* and everyone has to **STOP!** Shout, *'GREEN LIGHT'* then they can move again. Phew! Shout, *'PENGUIN'* and who knows what will happen?!

THE FLOOR IS LAVA

Do not touch the floor. The floor is lava. If you touch the floor you will be swallowed up by the fiery furnace of, well, lava.

Place helpful obstacles so you can get from one side of the game space to the other without touching the floor (because, remember, **LAVA! HOT LAVA! ARGH!**).

MARCO POLO

Now, this game can get very, very noisy.
Like, REALLY noisy. So play in a VERY BIG
OUTDOOR SPACE where you're not going
to annoy anyone!

You need one person to start as **'it'**. Blindfold
the volunteer, spin them around, then run away
and hide. Now the fun starts! The seeker shouts
'MARCO', and hiders shout **'POLO'**. In order to
find the hiders, the seeker follows the sound of
'POLO'. If the seeker finds you, you're it!

Even sillier? *Use a much smaller space and give
the seeker a blindfold. No hiding this time!*

WIDE GAMES

Now, these games are truly epic. You need a lot of space and a lot of people. And plenty of time. This game can last all afternoon!

Generally, loads of people are divided up into two teams and you're trying to capture something belonging to the other team.

Turn the page and try to . . .

. . . CAPTURE THE FLAG

Decide on two team bases and set up a flag midway between the bases. Within your teams, work out a strategy to capture the flag. Sounds simple? **Er . . . no!** The other team is plotting to **FOIL YOUR PLAN** the entire time.

Players can be captured if they are caught inside the other team's area. A captured players will have to do a forfeit – something **silly**, of course!

Top tip: Why not try a 'faint', where you send one or two runners out one way to tempt your opponents out of hiding, then everyone else runs and grab that flag. Good luck!

TREE-HEE

Another classic wide game. Start with
a biiiiiig space. Like, if you're camping,
use the WHOLE camping ground!

Find a tree. Preferably a big one. You know,
the one in your local park you call **THE** tree.

Split everyone into two teams. One team hides,
the other seeks. If you are caught, go wait by the
tree. Once everyone is caught, teams switch sides
and start again.

BUT if one of the hiding team gets back to the
tree without being caught, and touches the bark,
EVERY SINGLE caught person is freed again to
go and hide!

my favourite trees are
apple trees pear trees and
football common trees
ha ha do you get it

PORT, STARBOARD

'Port' and 'starboard' are fancy ship names for left and right. So, close your eyes for a moment and imagine you are on a ship. Like, a big old pirate ship . . . Got the picture in your mind?

Open your eyes. You are on a ship!

The four ends of a ship are:

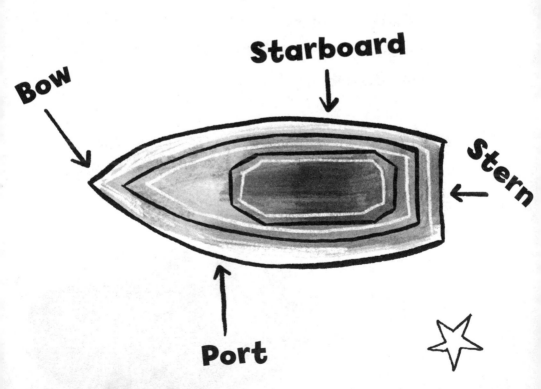

Set walls or outdoor boundaries for these areas. (OK, fine, you could use 'north, south, east and west' as directions instead, but then you wouldn't be on a pretend boat and that's less fun.) Choose a **'caller'** who shouts 'port', etc. Everyone else has to run to the right place. Last one there is out!

There are loads of other instructions to call – and the last one to do them is out:

Captain's coming! – everyone freezes, salutes, and says, 'Aye, aye, Captain!'

Climb the rigging! – run on the spot and grab imaginary ropes with your hands.

Lifeboats of three! – grab two friends and sit on the floor in a 'lifeboat'. The caller could also call 'four', 'five' . . . or any number of people.

Scrub the decks! – get down and pretend to wash those yucky, mucky ship floors. Ew!

THE HUNT

Tree-hee without the **tree** and without the hiding. Split into two teams: chasing and escaping. Once an escapee is caught, they become a chaser. The game ends when one last escapee is being chased by **EVERYONE ELSE.**

In my house, we made a Crystal Maze with different obstacle courses and puzzles in different rooms. If you don't get the answer in time, you get locked in the room! Although not really, because there aren't any keys.

Kylo, aged 8

On my birthday, my mum hid my presents around the house. But it was OK because she gave me clues. Everybody helped but the presents were all for me.

Reuben, aged 7

There is an apple tree near my house and sometimes I play Splat the Apple with my brothers. When the apples are rotten, you throw them and try to hit them with a cricket bat. Hahahah!

Zack, aged 9

Me and my sister pretend my dad is a crocodile. His legs are the mouth and he tries to catch us by snapping them shut. My sister got caught LOADS!

Erin, aged 7

if a crocodile married a frog and they had a baby then the baby would be called a croakodile ha ha

My family has a really silly game. You tie a new toilet brush round your waist with some string. It's clean! Then you set up some obstacles and you put a tennis ball on the floor. You use the toilet brush to dribble the ball between the obstacles to the finish line. The winner is the person who does it fastest. It's funny!

Lori, aged 11

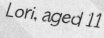

Once we played the chocolate game but with a banana. I had to peel it with a knife and fork which was SO HARD. It got really squishy.

Noah, aged 9

Apple bobbing is my favourite game at Halloween.

Zadie, aged 6

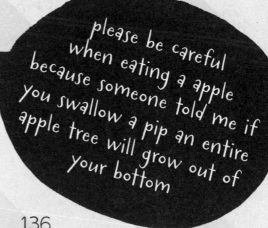

please be careful when eating a apple because someone told me if you swallow a pip an entire apple tree will grow out of your bottom

The doughnut game is my favourite! We try to eat jam doughnuts without licking our lips. It's hard because all the sugar gets stuck on them.

Mika, aged 10

We play the Yes No game in the car. I added a new category: NYES. Ha ha ha!

Raheem, aged 9

Do you know the game where you don't step on the cracks? I played it with my friend Yasmeen and when I stepped on a crack, she tickled me!

Jessie, aged 8

The staring game is my favourite. You need to stare at someone without blinking for as long as you can. The first person to blink or look away loses. Hahaha! I also like rhyme time, where you look for things in your house that rhyme, like cat and mat. The first person to find three rhymes is the winner. It's funny if you find rude things!

Elliott, aged 7

You know Pooh Sticks? Well, it's better with leaves because they are easier to spot. I guess it's called Pooh Leaves then?

Maeve, aged 8

I play Guess Who? with my little sister. We guess animals and the answer is ALWAYS giraffe. I don't know why!

Charlie, aged 10

GAMES THAT GOT TOO SILLY

actually i dont think you should read this chapter because its a bit too silly but then again if you bought a silly book and it wasnt silly enough that would be silly also

SILLIEST SPORTS

You can be a good sport, but then there's being a silly sport . . .

Did you know?

The highest **JENGA** tower ever was 397cm (almost four metres)! That's higher than a bungalow.

Guess what Ern Rubik invented? Scrabble. No! The **RUBIK'S CUBE!** After he'd invented it, it took him a **WHOLE MONTH** to solve it. Doh! There are **MANY** Rubik's world records, including the number of cubes solved underwater in one go (nine) and number solved while running 5km (77).

Did you know, singer **Justin Bieber** can solve a Rubik's Cube in under two minutes?

In May 1983, four American best friends started playing **TAG.** In 2017, aged over 40, they were **STILL PLAYING.** Yes, they never stopped! Even sillier? One member of the group, Jerry, **NEVER** got tagged. Very, very, VERY silly? Someone made a film about it!

In 2013, Silvio Sabba, from Italy, claimed the world record for stacking dice into a tower. He stacked 28 dice in one minute.

cor that sounds a bit dicey ha ha

GAMES GONE WRONG!

Of course, games can easily go WRONG. And sometimes it's VERY funny . . . for the people watching, at least!

PUPPY POWER

In the 1962 Football World Cup quarter final between England and Brazil, a dog invaded the pitch. The referee stopped play, but no one could catch the dog!

Eventually England striker Jimmy Greaves picked up the dog – which weed on him. **Yuck!** Back then, players didn't even bring spare shirts to matches so he had to play with dog wee all over him. **STINKY!**

BUM HOCKEY

In 2018, during an ice hockey match between two top American teams, St Louis Blues and Florida Panthers, a goal was disallowed that would have equalized the score. **Why?** It bounced off the referee's **bottom** before going straight into the goal! You're not allowed to deflect off the derrière. Hehehe!

JOUST SAY NO!

In 1536, Henry VIII took part in a jousting match that went **horribly** wrong. (Jousting – you know? Where knights charged at each other on horseback carrying **enormous** pointy sticks? **Yeah – what could possibly go wrong there?**) Henry fell off his royal horse and landed badly. Ouch! Some of his courtiers said his personality totally changed afterwards, which 'joust' shows you . . . even kings need to be careful!

IT'S A FIX!

No games EVER went wrong for the Roman Emperor Commodus (176–192CE). He liked to fight as a gladiator in the Colosseum. In all, he performed 735 fights and **won** them all. He must have been an amazing gladiator.

AHEM.

In fact, it was because no one was allowed to beat the emperor! Have YOU ever played any games like that?!

SILLIEST TV GAME SHOWS

Nothing goes wrong on telly, of course.
Oh, wait . . .

THE NOT-SO-AMAZING RACE

In 2010, a popular American TV show called
The Amazing Race introduced a round where
contestants had to fire watermelons out of
a medieval slingshot. One slingshot misfired
and flew into a contestant's face. **OW!** They
never did THAT round again.

ATTACK OF THE GUNGE

Like gunge? Not everyone does! At least
one TV contestant has come out in
a serious allergic reaction to it and
a director once slipped on gunge
and broke his collar bone - ouch!

Gunge is also REALLY difficult to clean up. On *Dick and Dom in Da Bungalow*, they needed a new carpet for every show. That's how gungey it got! **Ew!**

I'M A CELEBRITY

When the TV crew went out to the jungle to build the set for the first show in 2002, they accidentally dug up some old human bones! **Oh no!** Get me out of here! Luckily it turned out that they were very old ostrich bones ... which look a LOT like human bones!

'i think they should rename this show 'i am not actually that much of a celebrity to be honest and i would like to become more of one so please let me stay in here'

MORE *I'M A CELEBRITY* MADNESS

In one bushtucker trial alone, 1.5 MILLION flies were used. Singer Brian Harvey was BUZZED to take part in that one!

In the German version of the show, celebrities have to eat DOUBLE the amount of 'food' and 'drink' in the bushtucker trials, compared to the UK version. Bleurgh!

Once, the crew ran out of spiders so they put out a call asking local spider-hunters to collect them. They paid almost £3 per spider – that's super silly!

Silliest of all? The producers of the first series tried to ban loo roll! Understandably, the contestants revolted!

THE SILLIEST GAME OF ALL TIME

you have been warned this
is very very very very very
very very silly in fact i am
going to add another very
just to make sure you truly
see how silly it is there i
done it

Name: *TASKMASTER*

Origin: It started as a late-night comedy show where comedian Alex Horne challenged his friends to do silly things. It was **SO SILLY**, it got made into a primetime TV show.

How to play: Comedians Alex Horne and Greg Davies set tasks for a panel of comedians and celebrities. The winner is the person who has completes the task in the **SILLIEST** way! Some top telly tasks have been:

- Fill an egg cup with your own tears
- Blowing out a candle from the longest distance
- Bring a video game to life

AND NOW IT'S YOUR TURN!

You can easily and very, **VERY** silly-ly play
Taskmaster with your friends and family.
Over the page are some tasks to try at home . . .
and I bet you can think of much sillier ones!

Remember, there aren't any rules. So . . .

IT *WILL* GET SILLY!

SUPER SILLY CHALLENGES

How many can you complete?

MAKE YOUR
BATHROOM INTO
A DISCO

BECOME A SUPERHERO,
DEMONSTRATE YOUR
SUPERPOWERS

DRAW A PICTURE -
WITHOUT USING PENS
OR PENCILS

PERFORM A FAIRY TALE
USING YOUR FINGERS
OR TOES

TRAVEL THROUGH
TIME
(BUT . . . HOW?!)

DO SOMETHING
SURPRISING WITH
A HAT

MAKE MUSIC USING
JUST THINGS
THAT ARE IN YOUR
BEDROOM (NOT
INCLUDING MUSICAL
INSTRUMENTS!)

MAKE A VERY TINY
SANDWICH . . .
AND SERVE IT ON
A VERY BIG PLATE

COLLECT SOMETHING FROM
ENGLAND, IRELAND AND
SCOTLAND AND WALES FROM
AROUND YOUR HOUSE

MATT LUCAS

MATT LUCAS is an actor, writer, comedian and very silly person. He became famous by playing a big baby who played the drums in a crazy TV show called *Shooting Stars*. His next TV show after that was called *Little Britain*, which he did with David Walliams. *Little Britain* was very rude indeed and you are not allowed to watch it until you are at least 75 years old.

Matt has played lots of other characters on TV, including Mr Toad in *The Wind in the Willows*, Bottom in *A Midsummer Night's Dream* (ha ha, I just said bottom) and the companion Nardole in *Doctor Who*, although

156

it was too scary for Matt to watch. He has also appeared in some Hollywood films, such as *Paddington*, and *Alice in Wonderland*, where he played Tweedle Dee and his equally silly brother, Tweedle Dum. Matt has also done voices for several cartoons, including Benny in *Gnomeo and Juliet*. Recently Matt has been presenting on *The Great British Bake Off* and he keeps putting on weight because he eats all of the cakes. He has also been writing and singing about his friend Baked Potato. This book of games is his fifth super silly book for children.

As a child, Matt's favourite game was The Chocolate Game, which he loved so much, he went on to invent The Crisps Game, The Ice Cream Game and The Yorkshire Pudding With Lots of Gravy Game.

SARAH HORNE

SARAH HORNE is an illustrator and writer. She first learned to draw aged nine, when she needed to explain to the hairdresser how she wanted her hair to be cut. The result was not what she had hoped for – but her picture was pretty amazing, even if she says so herself.

Since aged nine, Sarah's drawing has got better and better (and so have her haircuts). She has illustrated over 70 books, including *Charlie Changes into a Chicken* and *Fizzlebert Stump: The Boy Who Ran Away From the Circus (and Joined the Library)*, *Puppy Academy*, and *Ask Oscar* and its sequels. Most of the books she has drawn have been very, very silly.

As a child, Sarah liked to play Kim's Game and The Chocolate Game. Her very favourite game was Lighthouses, which is played in a dark room with a torch and lots of chairs. One person shines the torch around the room like a lighthouse, and everybody else moves around, trying not to get spotted by the beam of light. Gotcha, Sarah!